THIS BOOK BELONGS TO ME

My name is ....

Attach a
photograph
of yourself here

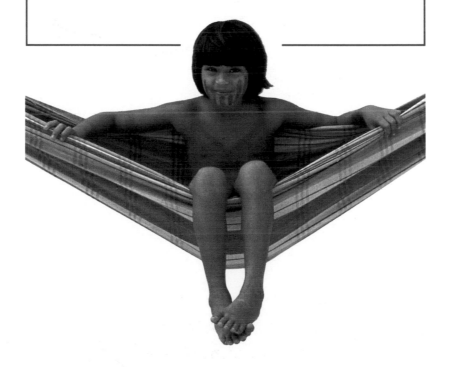

Our Favorite Stories

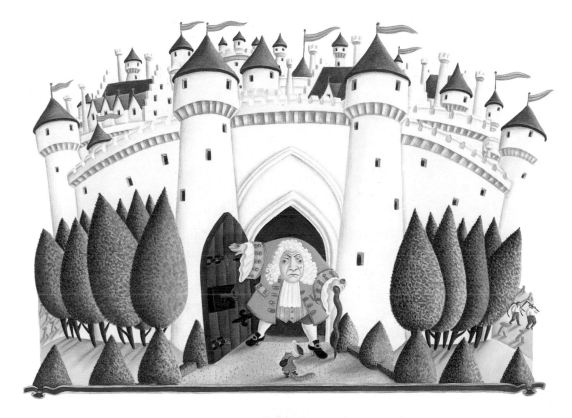

WRITTEN BY JAMILA GAVIN

ILLUSTRATED BY AMANDA HALL

PHOTOGRAPHY BY BARNABAS KINDERSLEY

A DK PUBLISHING BOOK

Compiled and edited by Miriam Farbey

Senior Designer Paula Burgess   **Picture Research** Joanne Beardwell

Research Jo Fletcher-Watson   **Americanization** Camela Decaire

Production Katy Holmes   **DTP Designer** Kim Browne

First American Edition, 1997
2 4 6 8 10 9 7 5 3 1

Published in the United States by DK Publishing, Inc.
95 Madison Avenue, New York, New York 10016
Visit us on the World Wide Web at http://www.dk.com

Published in Great Britain by Dorling Kindersley Ltd.

Ancient Art & Architecture 41cr; Ardea/ Kenneth Fink 46 clb; The Bridgeman Art Library 42bl, / Board of Trustees of the V&A 43cra;
Christie's Images 23cl; Bruce Coleman Collection/Jeff Foott Productions 18cra, /Luiz Marigo 10cla, /Mike Price 10flb; Colorific!/Jose Azel/Aurora 30cl; Ecoscene/Julie Meech
29cl; The Environmental Picture Library/Jed Booth 8br; Mary Evans Picture Library 21bl; 32bc; Robert Harding Picture Library/Walter Rawlings 15clb, Cybil Sassoon 35cr;
The Hutchison Library 37cr, 38cl 7bl; The Image Bank/Dann Coffey 24cr; Image Select/Ann Ronan 20tr; Instituto Nacional de Anthropologiae Historia/Michel Zabe 6tr,
7tr, 14tr & 15cla; Frank Lane Picture Agency/ FW Lane 10bl; Magnum/ Ernst Haas 15cl; NHPA/B&C Alexander 25bl,/Nigel J. Dennis 29cla, /EA Janes 43cr, /Haroldo Palo
10tl, /David Woodfall 10c; New Zealand Tourism Board 46cl; Panos Pictures/Jim Holmes 27cl; Ann & Bury Peerless 36bl & br, 37br; Planet Earth/Richard Coomber 41tr,
/Nikita Ovsyanikov 16cl, /David A Ponton 16bl; South American Pictures/Tony Morrison 9bl; Viewfinder 31br; Vireo/J. Dunning 6tl, 10fclb; Zefa 47tr, /Minden/F. Lanting 28cr.

A catalog record for this book is available from the Library of Congress.

ISBN 0-7894-1486-4

Color reproduction by Bright Arts
Printed and bound by New Interlitho, Italy

Contents

Introduction

All over the world children love stories. They inherit a huge storehouse from the religion, history, and folk traditions of their cultures. The stories in this book come from all corners of the globe: a folktale from Finland, a creation myth from the Canadian Inuit, a religious story from India. The roots of each story lie deep in spiritual or cultural ground. The themes will be recognized everywhere: the battle between good and evil, the perils of disobedience and disrespect for nature, the importance of bravery and wisdom. Full of mystery, wit, and wisdom, these tales have survived hundreds of years of retellings to become *Our Favorite Stories*.

ARI
is from Finland. He and his family are Saame people. He is taught about Saame culture at school, and knows many Saame folktales.

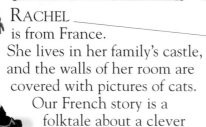

RACHEL
is from France. She lives in her family's castle, and the walls of her room are covered with pictures of cats. Our French story is a folktale about a clever cat, Puss-in-boots.

Arctic Circle

Finland

EUROPE

France

Morocco

AFRICA

India

Botswana

HOUDA
lives in the old walled fortress of the ancient town of Salé in Morocco. Our Moroccan story is about a king who, long ago, built a city to rival Paradise.

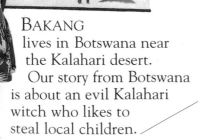

BAKANG
lives in Botswana near the Kalahari desert. Our story from Botswana is about an evil Kalahari witch who likes to steal local children.

MEENA
is from India. She is a Hindu, and our Indian story is one of the most important religious stories about the Hindu gods and goddesses. It tells of the birth of Krishna.

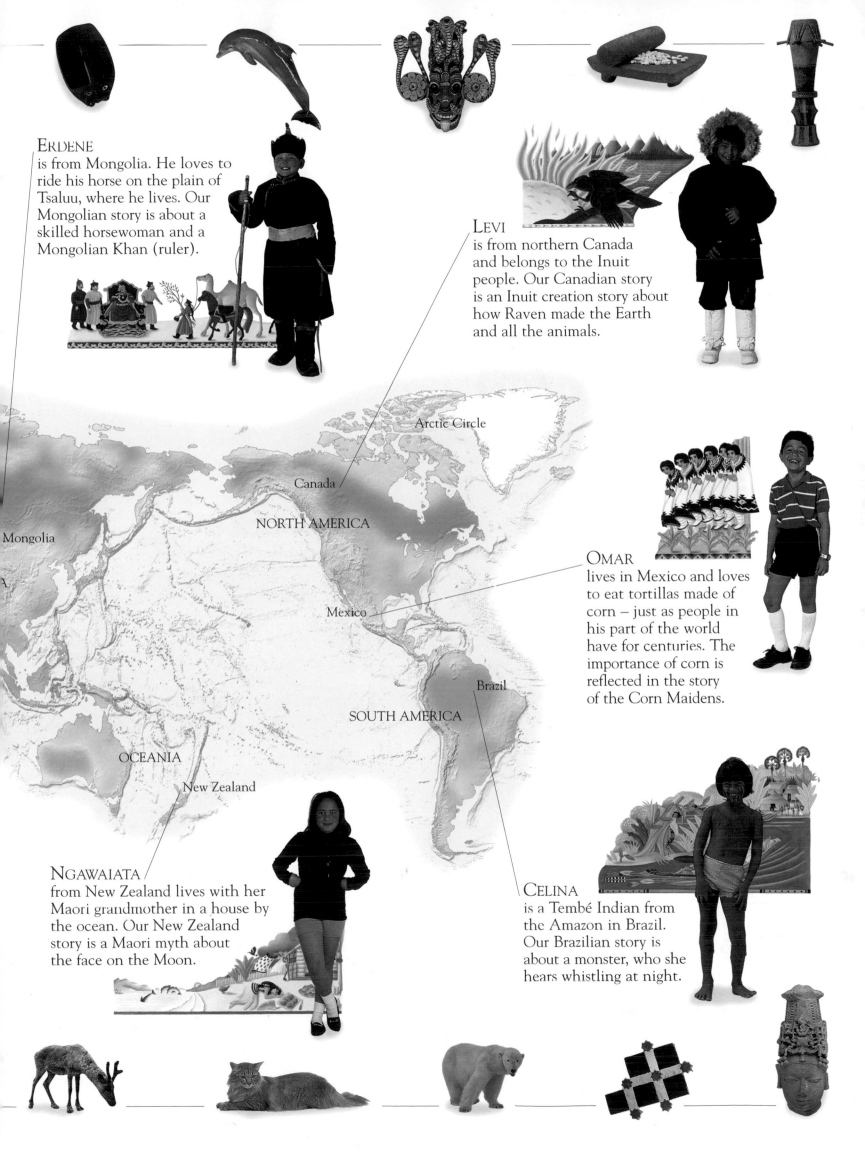

ERDENE is from Mongolia. He loves to ride his horse on the plain of Tsaluu, where he lives. Our Mongolian story is about a skilled horsewoman and a Mongolian Khan (ruler).

LEVI is from northern Canada and belongs to the Inuit people. Our Canadian story is an Inuit creation story about how Raven made the Earth and all the animals.

OMAR lives in Mexico and loves to eat tortillas made of corn – just as people in his part of the world have for centuries. The importance of corn is reflected in the story of the Corn Maidens.

NGAWAIATA from New Zealand lives with her Maori grandmother in a house by the ocean. Our New Zealand story is a Maori myth about the face on the Moon.

CELINA is a Tembé Indian from the Amazon in Brazil. Our Brazilian story is about a monster, who she hears whistling at night.

Arctic Circle

Canada

NORTH AMERICA

Mongolia

Mexico

Brazil

SOUTH AMERICA

OCEANIA

New Zealand

CELINA
Celina Tembé lives in the Amazon rain forest in Brazil. She loves living there, but is sometimes scared of an imaginary beast that whistles in the rain forest.

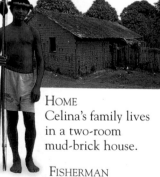

HOME
Celina's family lives in a two-room mud-brick house.

FISHERMAN
Like Kanassa in the story, Celina's brother Sergio goes fishing with a bow and arrow.

THE AMAZON RIVER
The world's second longest river, the Amazon winds through Brazil's rain forest.

The Whistling Monster

DEEP IN THE FOREST, where wonderful creatures creep, crawl, swoop, and shimmer, where the Amazon River winds like a great serpent, lived a boy called Kanassa.

Kanassa was always boasting: how he climbed the highest trees looking for honey, how no one in his village was more skillful than he at catching fish. He often aimed his arrows at the birds of the forest – the parrots and toucans and cockatoos – which annoyed them very much.

Kanassa loaded his canoe and set off up the great river.

8

One day a huge silver fish was sighted upriver.

"I'll catch that fish!" boasted Kanassa.

"Oh, Kanassa!" wailed his mother.

"Oh, Kanassa!" wailed his sister.

"Oh, Kanassa!" wailed his old grandmother. "Don't go too far up the river, or the Whistling Monster might get you."

Kanassa laughed. "Don't worry! I'm not afraid of monsters!"

He painted his face and body to show he was brave. He filled a *cabaça* with fresh water and stored bananas and gourds in his canoe. Then, taking his bow and his sharpest arrows, Kanassa paddled away upriver.

He paddled for three days, but there was no sign of the fish. Then, on the fourth day, he spotted it – shining like a moon and big enough to feed a village.

Kanassa stood, feet apart, the canoe so perfectly balanced there was not one ripple in the water. He fitted an arrow to his bow and aimed. Just as he was about to let fly, from out of the forest came a long, low, eerie whistle. The sound froze his blood. He fell back terrified.

Rising through the trees, he saw a coil of smoke. Kanassa paddled ashore.

"Someone in this village might know who made that strange noise."

He walked deep into the forest till he came to a group of mud huts. An old man was sitting nearby.

"Please, sir, what creature is it making that whistling sound?" asked Kanassa.

The old man looked scared. "Go home, boy! Go home. No one who crosses the path of the Whistling Monster lives to tell the tale."

The old man told Kanassa to beware the Whistling Monster.

WATER CARRIER
Celina carries water in a *cabaça*, like the one in the story. This is a dried-out, hollowed forest fruit.

BODY PAINTING
Tembé Indians like Celina and Kanassa decorate their bodies with red paint made from the *urucum* plant. Celina paints her body every day.

Red body paint made from crushed seeds

FRUITS OF THE FOREST
Banana plants grow in the rain forest. They have 10-20 leaves up to 11.5 ft (3.5 m) long. A large flower spike grows clusters of up to 150 bananas.

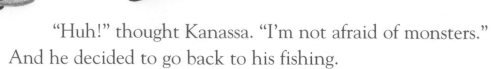

BIRDS OF THE AMAZON
One-fifth of all the different types of birds in the world live with Celina in the Amazon.

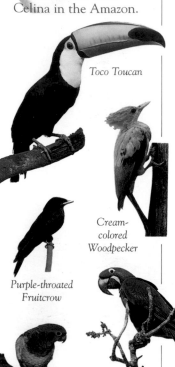

Toco Toucan

Cream-colored Woodpecker

Purple-throated Fruitcrow

Blue-headed Parrot

Hyacinth Macaw

Hoatzin

Campo Oriole

Sun Parakeet

Fork-tailed Flycatcher

Fork-tailed Woodnymph

Scarlet Macaw

"Huh!" thought Kanassa. "I'm not afraid of monsters." And he decided to go back to his fishing.

On the way back, the forest got darker and darker. His feet padded through the undergrowth. Other footsteps followed him. Kanassa stopped and listened. The footsteps stopped. Then he heard the whistling, not far away. Kanassa began to run. The footsteps behind him ran, too. The whistling got louder; he could almost feel its breath in his ear. Kanassa fell in terror behind a banana plant and pulled its leaves around him. Then he saw it. It was horrible. It was worse than anything the elders of the village had ever warned him of. It was wildly hairy; tall as a giant, with claws instead of hands and a terrible tail that thrashed around. But worst of all was the hole in its head. From out of the hole came the whistling sound.

Kanassa shivered. Kanassa shook. The leaves rattled with his fear. The monster saw him.

"Run, Kanassa, run!" screamed a voice in his head.

Kanassa ran. The monster followed, crashing and thundering behind him. The terrible whistling got closer and closer and closer.

"Help me! Help me!" yelled Kanassa to anyone who would hear him. The birds of the forest heard him.

"Why should we help you? You only aim arrows at us!"

"I promise I never will again!" pleaded Kanassa.

So the birds decided to help.

They flew in like a mighty wind, fluttering, pecking, and scratching. They ripped out the monster's hair and clawed his eyes. Kanassa ran and ran until he reached the river. He scrambled into his canoe and floated away. Above him, the birds wheeled like a rainbow.

"Thank you!" cried Kanassa.

"No fish?" scoffed the people when he returned.

"No fish," mumbled Kanassa. "But I saw the Whistling Monster and lived to tell the tale."

Fabulous birds flew in from every corner of the sky to attack the monster.

OMAR
Omar Salazar lives in Mexico near the coastal town of Cancún. Mexico was once home to the Pueblo Indians, who tell this story.

OMAR'S FAMILY
Like Omar's family, most Mexicans are of mixed Spanish and native Indian descent. Spanish settlers arrived in Mexico in the 1500s.

CORN
Omar eats a lot of tortillas, pancakes made of corn meal. Corn has always been a vital crop for the people of North America.

The Corn Maidens

LIFE, TILL THEN, HAD BEEN HARD. Sometimes the sun burned so fiercely the ground cracked. The rain didn't fall for months on end and the streams dried up. Worst of all, the corn didn't grow, and the people nearly starved. Then the Corn Maidens came: six sisters, dancing hand in hand in the fields. Their bare feet thudded in the deep furrows of the earth and they turned their glistening faces to the sky and sang "Come Sun! Come rain! Make the corn grow."

The Sun shone for them and the rain rained. The corn grew tall and the villagers reaped an abundance of corn.

"Stay with us forever," begged the villagers. "We will build you a house, and feed you, and we will always respect you."

So every year the Corn Maidens

→ *The Corn Maidens danced in the fields.*

danced in the fields and every year the corn grew tall. But as the people grew prosperous, they became neglectful. One year the Corn Maidens danced, but the people forgot about leaving them any food and stopped being respectful. The Corn Maidens were saddened, then angry. The eldest sister, Yellow Corn, said, "We must leave this place. Let the people see what happens when we are not here."

Before the mists of morning had lifted, the six Corn Maidens took the road south. They went to Pautiwa, the spirit man. "Please hide us until the people have learned they cannot prosper without us."

Pautiwa led the six Corn Maidens to the shores of a shining water and transformed himself into a duck. Drawing the sisters under one wing, he sank with them to the bottom of the lake.

Pautiwa and the Corn Maidens sank into the lake.

At first the villagers didn't notice that the Corn Maidens had gone. They carried on, confident that the corn would flourish as usual. But when the harvest came, the crop was poor. The next year it was worse. The year afterward it failed altogether.

The people went to their priest. "Help us!" they cried. "Even though the Sun shone and the rain came, our corn withered. What can we do?"

"Where are the Corn Maidens?" asked the priest.

The villagers looked around. "We didn't need them any more. All they did was dance. We were the ones who worked day and night in the fields. They must have gone."

"Find them," ordered the priest.

Paiyatuma sat encircled by many butterflies.

CLAY FLUTE
The flute was popular throughout North America. It was often played at religious ceremonies.

PRAYER STICKS
Prayer sticks with feathers were used by many native Americans.

PUEBLO HOMES
Pueblo people lived in mud-brick complexes several stories high, with interconnecting rooms.

The villagers searched in every direction, but in vain. Then someone said, "We must go to Paiyatuma, the magic musician. Only he can help us."

Paiyatuma lived high among the rocks near the head of a waterfall, beneath the arch of an everlasting rainbow. As the people toiled up the hill they heard him playing his flute. His music was magic. Nothing could resist its power. Paiyatuma sat crowned with flowers and encircled by butterflies.

"Oh, Paiyatuma, oh, most gracious musician, blessed by the gods, we are starving because the Corn Maidens have run away. Please help us find them."

Paiyatuma prepared four prayer sticks: yellow, red, blue, and white. To each he fixed an eagle's feather, then set them facing the north, south, east, and west. Although the wind blew, the feathers on the yellow, blue, and white sticks stayed still, but the feather on the red stick swayed to and fro.

"Ah!" smiled Paiyatuma. "Your maidens went south. Their breath moves the feather. I'll take you to them."

Putting his flute to his lips, Paiyatuma led the villagers south, playing all the way. His notes dropped like pebbles through the shining waters of the lake, down to where the Corn Maidens lay sleeping.

Roller grinds seeds.

GRINDING THE CORN
Trays of seeds were a common sight in Pueblo villages. The seeds were ground to make corn meal.

The sisters awoke and wanted to dance. Pautiwa floated up with them to the surface of the lake. The people fell on their knees before the Corn Maidens and begged forgiveness. "Please come back with us," they cried. "Now we know how much we need you."

Pautiwa shook his feathers and changed back into human form, clothed in a flowing white cloak. "Yes," he told the maidens, "it is time for you to return."

Paiyatuma led the way, playing his flute. The Corn Maidens danced behind him, followed by the villagers. Pautiwa went last. They reached the village. There was such joy the celebrations lasted all night. But, just before dawn, the Corn Maidens placed a tray of seeds on the ground. Paiyatuma laid his flute next to it, then they slid away into the darkness.

"Do not fear!" Pautiwa comforted the villagers. "Here are corn seeds and Paiyatuma's flute. Choose six dancing maidens and I will stay until you have learned the music and the dances. If you perform them faithfully every year, the corn will always grow." As the villagers learned the songs and ceremonies, bit by bit, Pautiwa faded away like morning mist.

The villagers always after remembered the Corn Maidens, and their corn always grew tall.

The Corn Maidens and the villagers danced home.

The Coming of Raven

BEFORE THE CREATION OF THE WORLD, there was darkness black as Raven's wings. The darkness was Raven. Raven was Tulugaukuk, the Father of Life.

LEVI
Levi Eegeesiak lives in a remote town in northern Canada called Iqaluit. Levi is an Inuit. The Inuit were one of the first peoples of northern Canada.

THE ARCTIC SUN
Levi's town is so far north that it is in the Arctic Circle. In winter it is almost always dark. The Sun only rises for two hours a day, and the sea freezes over.

ARCTIC BEAUTY
During summer in the Arctic, the Sun shines all day long. It sustains a beautiful variety of plants and animals.

Raven felt the edges of his feathers singe as sparks from the Sun flew up into the air and lit up his creation.

Raven spread his wings and flew down from Skyland. With mighty thrusts of his wings, he created a land called Earth. As he swooped and soared, he created the mountains, the trees, and the rushing waters. Yet darkness was everywhere; black as everlasting night; black as Raven's wings. Raven longed to see his creation.

Something glinted in the ground. It was burning hot. When sparks from it flew into the air, Raven glimpsed oceans, glaciers, and great forests.

"With this rock, I will be able to see what I have made," cawed Raven joyfully. He plunged toward the fiery rock, clasped it in his claws, and threw it up in the sky. The rock was the Sun.

The Sun gave out a mighty light. Raven saw his marvelous creation – jungles, seas, deserts, and grasslands.

"Pop!" Raven turned in time to see a giant plant pod burst open. Out tumbled the first living creature. It was naked and frightened. It was a man, the first Inuit. The man crawled around and then stood on two legs and with two hands reached out for food to eat. He bawled loudly, "I am cold, I am hungry. I am lonely!"

"Oh, dear," sighed Raven, and created caribou, seal, whale, walrus, bear, and ox. Now the man could hunt for food and clothes.

"But I have no weapons to hunt with," cried the man.

"That's true," agreed Raven. "If I show you how to make a bow and arrows and a spear, will you promise not to kill more animals than you need to live?"

"I promise!" said the man.

So Raven showed the Inuit how to make a bow and arrows and a spear.

"And who will tend the fire while I'm away hunting? And who will keep me company through the long, cold nights?" wailed the man.

Raven flapped his wings and created a woman.

In time, there were more men and women, and they produced children. They chopped down forests to make houses; they made thread out of the sinews of animals, and needles from their bones. They killed more and more animals. The Earth, sea, and sky were plundered as the people became greedy, always wanting more.

CARIBOU
One animal Raven creates is the caribou, the wild reindeer of North America. Levi's father hunts caribou for meat.

The first man was born from a plant pod.

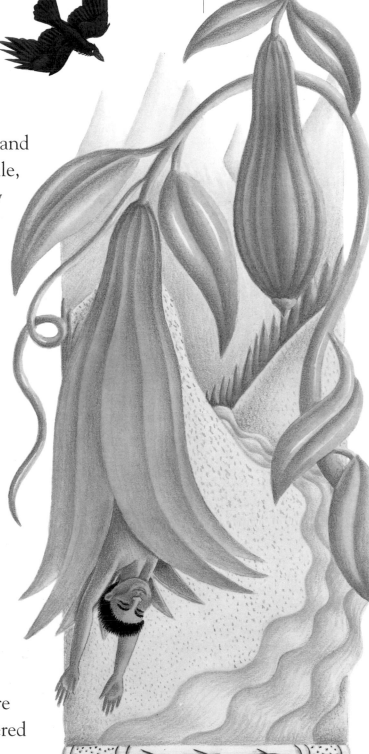

HUNTING
The Inuits in the story hunted with bows and arrows like these, or with harpoons (long spears).

The people forgot their promise to Raven and killed more and more animals.

Earth cried out in pain and Raven heard its cry.

"Don't you remember your promise, oh, Inuit people?" cawed Raven angrily. "Only to take what you need?"

But by this time the Inuit people no longer listened to Raven. They had forgotten their promise, and didn't care about anything except their own desires. So Raven took a bag made from caribou skin. He soared toward the Sun, grabbed it, stuffed it into the bag, and flew back to Skyland. The world was plunged into darkness.

*Raven Boy
hurled the Sun
across the sky.*

"Oh, oh, oh!" howled the Inuit. "We can't see, we can't keep warm, please give us back the Sun."

So every now and then Raven took pity on the people, and uncovered the Sun for a few days to allow them to hunt.

Now Raven thought he should have a companion. So he took Snow Goose to be his wife, and they had a son called Raven Boy. Sometimes Raven showed his son the caribou skin bag and the Sun inside it. Raven Boy became fascinated by the fiery rock.

One day, while his father was sleeping, Raven Boy crept up to the bag, determined to open it and see the Sun. But Raven woke up. Fearful of his father's anger, Raven Boy fled with the bag to the other side of the Universe and hid.

Below on Earth, without any sunshine at all, everything began to die.

"Please save us, oh, Raven, creator of the Universe. Give us back the Sun!" implored the Inuit.

Raven took pity and went to look for his son. He cawed, "Raven Boy! Don't hide. Bring back the Sun, or the world I created will die!"

Raven Boy heard his father's plea. He ripped open the bag and flung the Sun spinning across the sky.

But so that the Inuits would remember the terror of darkness, Raven created night and day, winter and summer. And the Inuit never forgot their promise again. Forever after, they respected all animals, and honored Raven.

ANIMALS IN DANGER
Recently Arctic animals have been over-hunted, as they were in the story. People in Europe and America want fur and other animal products. Some laws have been passed to limit hunting.

Newborn harp seals have white fur for camouflage on the ice.

Polar bears have thick fur to keep them warm.

Walruses rub mustaches.

Puss-in-boots

A MILLER HAD THREE SONS. He was so poor that when he died, all he had to leave to his sons was the mill to his eldest, a donkey to his second, and nothing to his third – except a cat.

"You're no use to me," said the youngest son to the cat. "I'm off to seek my fortune."

To the lad's amazement, the cat spoke. "Don't be in such a hurry! Give me some boots and a drawstring bag, and I'll make your fortune."

Puss set out to make a fortune.

Puss got his bag and his boots and scampered off into the fields. He stuffed the bag with lettuce leaves. Silly rabbit came by and poked his nose inside to nibble. In a flash, Puss pulled the drawstring tight. He took the rabbit straight to the king and said, "Your Majesty, my master, the Marquis of Carabas, begs you to accept this humble gift."

The king was pleased. So Puss came again the next day, this time with two partridges. The king was delighted at the loyal generosity of the Marquis of Carabas.

Puss's sharp ears overheard that the king and his daughter would be out driving by the river the next day. So Puss told the miller's son to go bathing in the river. "Why not?" thought the lad. Puss then hid his clothes and waited for the king to come by.

Clip, clop, clippety clop! The carriage was coming. Puss called out, "Stop! Help! My master is drowning!" When the king saw it was Puss, he ordered his servants into the river to save the Marquis.

"Oh, sire!" cried Puss. "Some villains stole my master's clothes while he bathed."

"Don't worry, I'll see to it." The king ordered a cloak to be thrown around the miller's son. Then he made room for him inside his coach.

RACHEL
Rachel Hubert is twelve years old. She lives in the countryside in the Bordelais region of France. Her favorite animals are cats.

THE CHÂTEAU
Rachel's home is a *château* (castle). It has been in her family since 1715. French noblemen, including Marquises, traditionally lived in grand *châteaux*.

CHARLES PERRAULT
Puss-in-boots is an old folktale, written down by Perrault in 1697. It shows that effort and cleverness are well rewarded.

The princess was enchanted – and immediately fell in love with the lad.

Back at the palace, the king provided the miller's son with a royal set of clothes. Now he did indeed look like the Marquis of Carabas in his velvet suit of lace and gold trimmings, his silken shirt, and leather boots up to his thighs. How spectacular was the fine-feathered hat!

"I insist on driving you home," said the king. "Where do you live?"

THE MILL
In a mill, wheat was ground to make flour for bread. Rats and mice liked to eat the wheat, so the miller kept a cat to catch them.

Puss begged the king to save his master from drowning.

21

"I can turn into anything,"
thundered the ogre.

HARVEST TIME
Every year
in fall, peasants
reaped, or cut,
ripe wheat for
landowners.
Today, Rachel
can see wheat
being harvested
by machines.

Sickle has hooked blade.

The miller's son groaned to himself, "That's it. The game's up. I'll lose my head for sure when he sees I don't live in a castle." But Puss replied, "My master lives in Carabas Castle. I shall go on ahead and prepare for Your Majesty's arrival."

On the way Puss crossed meadows, fields, and woods.

"If the king asks who owns all this land," he told the peasants, "just reply the Marquis of Carabas, or I'll have your guts for garters."

Then on he went to the huge castle on top of the hill. In time, the king came by with his daughter and the miller's son.

"Who owns all this?" he called to the peasants.

"It all belongs to the Marquis of Carabas," they dutifully replied.

"Everything I see belongs to you!" exclaimed the king, admiringly, and the miller's son gave a shy shrug.

Meanwhile, Puss had reached the castle. It really belonged to a frightful man-eating ogre who had magic powers. Puss went up bravely and hammered on the door.

"Who's there?" roared the ogre.

"Me. Puss. I've heard about your magic powers. But I don't believe it. Is it true you can turn yourself into anything?"

"Of course it's true!" thundered the ogre, opening the door.

"Show me!" challenged Puss.

He was such a boastful ogre. With one roar he became a lion. Puss leaped for his life onto the castle roof.

"Very good!" Puss clapped his paws. "But you can't go from being a mighty lion to a teeny weeny mouse, can you?"

"But of course," squeaked the ogre, instantly becoming a mouse.

"Got you!" cried Puss, who pounced and ate him up.

The miller's son could hardly believe it when the king's carriage pulled up in front of the huge castle and there was Puss, bowing and scraping as he welcomed in the king's party. He set them before a table groaning beneath a splendid banquet – which had actually been the ogre's supper.

THE BIGGEST AND SMALLEST
The lion and the mouse are frequently paired in folktales. In this story Puss persuades the ogre to show off the range of his magic powers. The ogre is tricked into turning himself into cat food.

Everyone feasted on the ogre's supper.

"Sir, I'd like you to marry my daughter," drooled the king, wiping the wine from his mouth.

"Sire, I'd be delighted," said the miller's son, who had fallen as much in love with the princess as she had with him.

So they married. And as for Puss, he got a new pair of boots and never chased mice again – except for fun.

The Simple Saame Man

A SAAME MAN LIVED IN the forest with his clever wife and his pretty daughter, Nastai. Being a simple fellow, the man was content to let his wife be in charge of everything. She knew where to hunt and fish, set the traps, and knot the nets; it was she who herded the reindeer, cured the furs, made the clothes, and cooked the meals and kept the fire going.

Nastai's mother fished in the lake.

One sad day Nastai's mother died. Now it was Nastai who had to do everything. So she did – and did it well.

Then one day a beggar woman and her daughter arrived. They had heard about the man who, despite being simple, did very well for himself. They plotted to get all he had for themselves.

One day Nastai came in from the forest to find the beggar woman and her daughter sitting on either side of the hearth as though they owned the place.

"Who are you?" gasped Nastai.

"I am now the mistress of the house and you'll do as I say."

"Father?" Nastai implored.

But her simple father just nodded helplessly.

"You see? He agrees. Now get to the stove and cook us our dinner," shrieked the beastly woman.

Nastai became their slave. She did everything for them and got nothing in return.

But the beggar woman hated Saame land. She hated the wind wailing in the forest; she hated the wolves howling at night; she hated the loneliness. But most of all she hated Nastai, who was as good and beautiful

ARI
Ari Laiti lives inside the Arctic Circle in northern Finland.
He and his family, like the family in the story, are Saame people.

WINTER DARKNESS
In the Arctic, the Sun hardly shines all winter. Winds whistle through the snowy forests. Ari dislikes this dark time.

ARI'S FISHING ROD
Like Nastai and her mother, Ari is a good fisherman.

REINDEER HERD
Nastai's family depended on its reindeer herds for food and clothing. Ari's half-brother Toni is a reindeer herder today.

SLEIGH
Saame people once traveled on sleighs pulled by reindeer. The narrow, wooden runners slid easily over snow.

SNOWMOBILES
Ari and his family round up reindeer traveling on snowmobiles, motorized sleighs on skis.

as the beggar woman's daughter was ugly and ill-tempered.

One day the beggar woman announced, "We're leaving!" She ordered the simple man to herd together the reindeer, prepare the sleigh, and stack it with every single thing in the hut. Then she and her daughter got in the back.

"What about me?" cried Nastai.

"Who wants you?" sneered the evil woman, and she ordered the simple man to whip up the reindeer and get going.

he beggar woman
rove off with Nastai's
ther and all their possessions.

Her mother's voice told Nastai how to catch a reindeer calf.

LAKE FULL OF FISH
Nastai fished in one of the thousands of lakes and rivers hidden in the Finnish pine forests. The waters are full of fish – Ari fishes in them for trout and salmon.

Trout

The hut was empty. Nastai wept, "They have taken the nets, traps, reindeer – and father, too. How will I live? They have taken everything."

"Not quite everything," said a soft voice.

"Mother?" exclaimed Nastai. She turned, but could see no one.

"Look around," said her mother's voice. "They left one thing behind."

Nastai searched high and low. What could it be? Then the Sun glinted on a single thread caught in the floorboards. She pulled at it. The more she tugged, the more it unraveled.

"Knot the thread and make a fishing net," said her mother. "Then cast it into the lake."

Nastai obeyed. To her joy, the net was soon jumping with fish. That night she ate a delicious fish stew.

"Now go into the forest and find a young pine. Braid its roots together and make a rope. Then catch a reindeer calf," said her mother's voice.

Nastai obeyed. She made a rope, caught a young reindeer, and tethered it outside the hut. The next morning she was astonished to find the reindeer's mother standing by her calf. The day after the buck came with a son, and soon the rest of the herd all gathered before Nastai's hut. Now Nastai had plenty of food, reindeer milk, and company.

Meanwhile, the beggar woman and her daughter had soon spent the simple man's wealth. Once more they were dirt poor and close to starving. They had only one reindeer left. The woman ordered the simple man to harness it up. "We shall go back to your hut. At least we'll have a roof over our heads. Nastai must be dead."

So back they all went. But what a surprise.

As they came near the hut, they saw a herd of reindeer grazing quietly, a coil of smoke spiraled from the chimney, and a delicious smell of cooking came through the open door. They burst inside. Nastai beamed all over at the sight of her father.

"Good!" exclaimed the beggar woman. "We have everything we need."

For the first time in his life, the simple man spoke and took charge.

"Oh, no, you don't! This is my hut. Get out, beggar woman, and take your horrible daughter with you."

He kicked the two of them out and slammed the door.

Nastai gave her father the best fish stew of his life, and from then on they lived in happiness.

MOTHER AND CHILD
A mother reindeer will look for her calf if it gets lost. She makes grunting noises and, when her calf answers, she follows the sounds until she finds it.

Nastai welcomed her father back home.

BAKANG
Bakang Gabankalafe
lives in a village
called Tshabong in
Botswana. Tshabong
is on the edge of the
Kalahari desert,
where the boys in
the story live.

THE KALAHARI DESERT
The Kalahari is very dry,
so cattle herders, like the
boys' and Bakang's father,
travel far into the desert
to find water for
their herds. In
the south are
the "Singing
Sands." Here,
a singing sound is heard
when sand is disturbed.

HOME
Bakang and her
mother live in a
house made of earth
and dried cow dung.

Witch of the Sands

ON THE FAR SIDE OF THE SINGING SANDS, where the sound of one step upon the shining white grains can be heard a hundred miles away, lived an evil witch who liked to steal children.

The herdsman built a tree house for his sons.

It was because of this witch that a desert herdsman decided to build a tree house for his three young, motherless sons. He built it high in the branches of an acacia tree and the only way up or down was by a rope ladder.

Every day the herdsman warned his sons, "While I'm away, don't let down the ladder to anyone except me. You will know when I come, for I will whistle three times."

The boys promised. So every day when their father herded his cattle into the desert to graze, the boys would scamper around among the branches, happy as can be. And every evening they let down the rope ladder when they heard their father whistle.

But one day the evil witch came, and sat in the deep shade of the acacia tree. She knew that, above her head, three pairs of eyes gazed down at her.

"Little boys," she croaked, "let down the ladder so I can come up and see your wonderful tree house."

But because they did not hear the whistle, the boys did not let down the ladder.

The wicked witch hid. The next evening when the father came home, she heard him whistle three times, and down tumbled the ladder.

"Ah-ha!" the witch gloated. "That's what I'll do!"
The boys told their father about the old woman. "Beware,"

Three pairs of eyes gazed down at the wicked witch.

he said. "It could have been the wicked witch of the Singing Sands."

The next day, when the father had gone into the desert, the witch came back. She whistled three times. Down came the ladder and the witch climbed up.

"Now I've got you!" she screamed and, tucking two boys under one arm and one under the other, she made off.

When the father came home, he saw the dangling ladder.

WITCH'S LOOKOUT
In Botswana, people believe that owls keep guard for wicked witches and warn them if someone is coming.

SPOTTED HYENA
Witches are said to ride around on the backs of hyenas. Hyenas are fierce, doglike hunters not afraid of attacking humans.

AFRICAN DRUMS
Some Africans believe drums have magic powers, like the drum in the story. Only important men, such as wise men, own drums. They can appoint people to play them.

Drum from Cameroon

Drum from Congo

MAGIC DISGUISE
In parts of Africa, body paint or ash may be worn to impart magic powers.

MAGIC STICKS
Traditional African healers use sticks to summon up healing spirits. Witches are thought to use sticks to summon up evil.

... wrapped a cloak around himself ...

He knew that something terrible had happened. The tree house was empty and his little boys gone. He thought his heart would break. He ran howling into the desert. "Has anyone seen my boys?"

The herdsman ran to the door of a wise man and fell at his feet. "Help me, help me! My three sons have disappeared. I fear they have been stolen by the wicked witch of the Singing Sands. What shall I do?"

"There is only one way to get them back and that is to kill her. There is only one way to kill her and that is to break her magic stick, in which all her powers lie. There is only one way to cross the Singing Sands without her hearing you, and that is to take my golden drum and beat it with this stick," the wise man said.

The herdsman rubbed ash in his hair to make it gray and hid the golden drum under a cloak. Disguised as an old man, he set off toward the Singing Sands.

When he got to that shining white place, before he put one foot upon the sands, he began to beat the magic drum. As soft as a heartbeat, he crossed the Singing Sands.

The herdsman rubbed ash in his hair...

On the other side he saw the witch's hut. He hobbled up to her door. "Oh! My aching stomach! Would a kind person have a crumb of food for a starving old man?"

"I didn't hear you coming," screamed the witch. "Begone!" But then she caught a glimpse of the golden drum beneath his cloak. She wanted it. "On second thoughts," she gave a crocodile smile, "I may have a morsel left over. Come on in."

... and set off to cross the Singing Sands.

30

The herdsman snapped the magic stick in two.

There was a cauldron bubbling, and the witch stirred it with her magic stick. Glowing in a dark corner were three pairs of frightened eyes, and the herdsman knew he had found his boys.

"Mmm! That smells good," he said, putting his nose into the steam.

"You can taste some when I've mixed in this powder," said the witch, thinking she could poison the old man and steal his drum. For a moment, she set down her magic stick to sprinkle in the poison. In that instant, the herdsman snatched up the stick and snapped it across his knee. The witch screamed, but before she could say a word, she crumbled into a pile of dust.

The herdsman joyfully hugged his sons and led them back across the shining white Singing Sands. He didn't bother to beat the golden drum. Everybody heard them coming and rejoiced.

WITCH'S BREW
In Botswana, witches are said to mix up local herbs to make powders that poison their victims or send them to sleep.

African oil palm herb

WHITE SANDS
Desert sands may be white because, years ago, streams carried minerals into the area that dried a bright white color.

The Paradise City

THERE WAS ONCE A KING who ruled over a vast and prosperous land. Not only was he wealthy beyond compare, but he had a beautiful wife, two noble sons, and a glorious palace, with courtyards and gardens that were the finest in the Arab world.

In his favorite courtyard, the king read about Paradise.

HOUDA
Houda Elazhar lives in Salé in Morocco. Houda and her family are Muslims. Muslims believe good people will go to a place called Paradise after death.

HOME
Houda lives in a traditional Moroccan-style home. Rooms are built around tiled courtyards, as they were in the king's palace.

KING OF MOROCCO
Morocco has been ruled by kings for over a thousand years. This story warns them to be humble.

But the king was not satisfied. He was sure he could have something better. He questioned scholars and wise men, he pored over manuscripts and books, he asked every visitor who passed through his city if they had seen a better kingdom than his.

"No, my lord," they invariably replied. "We have seen nothing to compare with this."

Then one day the king came across a huge, dusty book lying hidden in a corner of the library. He opened the book and began to read. He read about a place called Paradise. Nowhere was more beautiful than Paradise. It was more beautiful than anything on Earth, and it was where the good people went after death. The more he read,

The most precious materials were collected to adorn Paradise.

the more he tried to picture what Paradise was like. Surely the palaces in Paradise would be built from silver and gold with diamond-studded courtyards; the gardens would be running with cool streams, shaded by rare trees, and nodding with sweet-smelling flowers. Surely nowhere on Earth would be happier and more tranquil?

He was determined he would build such a place. He would create Paradise on Earth.

The king summoned his courtiers and noblemen, his architects and craftsmen, and ordered them to build him a city full of shimmering palaces and glorious courtyards. There must be palaces of light and air and water and marble, wood, gold, and silver, embedded with the finest metals and jewels. Towers and pinnacles should pierce the clouds, city walls should glitter with precious stones that could be seen from horizon to horizon. There must be gardens so perfumed that songbirds would fly in from every corner of the globe and never wish to leave.

"But, Sire," protested the chief architect, "you already have the finest city of palaces and gardens in all the world. How can we build anything better?"

The king roared, "Go and do as I have decreed!"

So the builders and craftsmen, architects, and laborers searched to the ends of the Earth to find the most precious materials the world could offer.

The king led
a procession
into the city of
jeweled palaces.

Bit by bit palaces went up –
a hundred of them – one for each of the
king's nobles. They had pillars of ruby and opal,
and floors inlaid with amber and amethyst. The rooms
shimmered with sapphire, topaz, tourmaline, and emerald.
The years went by, and still the building continued. The
gardens were laid out: fountains spouting perfume, streams running

with diamonds, and trees, shrubs, and flowers of such rare beauty that the songbirds sang like angels.

So involved was the king with building Paradise he hardly noticed when his wife died, and his sons went away to seek their fortunes, and his friends and advisors gradually withered away. When at last the city was complete, the king, now old, decreed there should be a magnificent opening ceremony.

He would go in procession to see his creation. With his armies, servants, and courtiers, he rode to the golden gates of his glorious city.

"Look!" he cried, his voice booming among the lonely towers. "Isn't this the most magnificent palace to be found anywhere on Earth or in Heaven?" The empty rooms echoed with his pride and arrogance.

"Have I not built Paradise itself?"

Barely had the words escaped his lips than the sky darkened. A dreadful sound rumbled below them, and the walls began to shake. The horses neighed and the people trembled.

"Look!" cried a voice shaking with fear.

Everyone stared in horror as the ground cracked and opened beneath their feet. The Paradise gardens, the wonderful palaces, the towers of the jeweled city, all the people and animals – everything – began to sink into the earth.

"My dream, my dream!" wept the greedy king, as he, too, was swallowed up.

Nothing remained. Not one shrub or songbird or bubbling stream; not one minaret or glittering jewel or marble stone. Nothing was left of the Paradise city but the desert sands shifting over the traces, and the wind moaning over the dunes.

The beautiful city was swallowed up forever.

SPARKLING JEWELS
The king used the most beautiful, rare, and weather-resistant stones, crystals, and gems in the world to build his city.

Diamonds

Amber

Marble

Sapphire

Tourmaline

Topaz

Opal

Emerald

Amethyst

Ruby

Ruby spinel

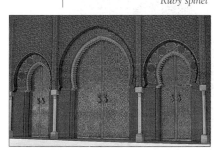

GOLDEN GATES
Morocco still has many fine palaces. These are the Dar Asselam Gates of the royal palace in Fès.

The Birth of Krishna

KANSA WAS A WICKED KING who lived long ago. One day he was told by a soothsayer that he would be killed by the eighth child born to his sister, Devaki. Kansa was outraged and had Devaki and her husband, Vasudeva,

Wicked Kansa had Devaki and Vasudeva thrown into dungeons in chains.

guarded day and night. He ordered that any baby born be destroyed, and Devaki's first seven children were killed at birth.

Kansa hoped to keep his evil plan a secret. He threatened to kill his guards if any of them said a word. He didn't want the gods to hear of it. But they did. Lord Vishnu, the Preserver, the God of Goodness and Mercy, who has the power to be born again many times and in many ways, decided he would be born as Devaki's eighth child, and went to become Devaki's embryo baby.

When Devaki's eighth child was due to be born, Kansa took no chances. He had Devaki and Vasudeva thrown into the dungeons. An armed guard was placed, day and night, outside the locked door.

It was the middle of the night. A strange calm hung over the world. It was so still that not even a breath of wind stirred the dusty ground. Devaki cried out. The dark, moist body of a boy wriggled into the world and the Universe shivered with excitement. In Heaven, drums thudded wildly. Lord Indra scattered a shower of flowers and raindrops out of the sky. Goddesses, angels, nymphs, and holy men burst out singing. "Lord Vishnu has been born again as a Man, and his name is Krishna!"

Vasudeva held his son fearfully. How could he save their baby?

Suddenly, Krishna opened his eyes. It was like the windows of Heaven opening; it was like a key turning in a lock. Devaki and Vasudeva

MEENA
Meena lives with her family in the Indian capital city of New Delhi. Meena is a Hindu. Hindus worship Vishnu and other gods.

PRESERVER GOD
Vishnu keeps the balance of good and evil in the Universe. When evil has the upper hand, he is reborn to restore goodness. His earthly forms are called "avatars." Krishna is his eighth avatar.

Devaki

Vasudeva

HOLY TEXT
The story of Krishna's birth is told in the popular religious work the *Bhagavata-Purana*.

were amazed as the chains fell from their bodies and the prison door flew open. Outside, the guards were slumped in deep slumber.

"Quick! Save our baby!" whispered Devaki. The tears streamed down her face, for she longed to keep him and nurse him and kiss him.

Vasudeva held baby Krishna above his head as the waters rose higher.

For a moment, the family embraced, then Vasudeva fled with his son into the night.

He ran till he came to the banks of the Yamuna River. If only he could get across, they would be safe, for on the other side lived a cowherd and his wife, Nanda and Yasoda. They were good, honest people who would care for Krishna as if he were their own child.

Vasudeva waded into the water. He was halfway across when a storm blew up. The waters churned angrily. Soon Vasudeva had to hold his baby high above his head.

THE YAMUNA RIVER
The Yamuna River flows through Meena's home city of New Delhi on its way to join the sacred Ganges River.

COWHERD
Baby Krishna, Nanda, and Yasoda appear in many beautiful little Indian paintings, called miniatures.

*Krishna was brought up as
the son of Nanda, a cowherd.*

He thought the end had come and they must both drown when Krishna stretched out a toe and dipped it into the waves. Miraculously, the swirling waters dropped away, and Vasudeva waded safely out on the other side.

Nanda and Yasoda took the baby. "Don't worry," they murmured. "We will treasure him like a god." Vasudeva thanked them and returned to his wife.

So Krishna was brought up as the son of a cowherd.

He romped and played, and was good and bad like any other human child. Sometimes he was very naughty. His name could be heard, ringing out across the meadows. "Krishna is a naughty boy! Krishna is stealing milk from the milkmaids and butter from their churns! Krishna is hanging on to cows' tails so they can drag him through the grass!"

"Is it true, Krishna?" his mother would ask, and he would flash his black eyes and peal with laughter so that his pearly teeth shone like stars. No one could be angry with him for long.

Yasoda hoped and feared for him like any mother. She warned him of dangers, like the demon ogress who ate children and the *naga* who lived on the riverbank.

One day the village children rushed up to Yasoda and told her that Krishna had been eating chalk.

"Is it true? Have you been eating chalk?" she asked.

"No, it's not true," declared Krishna. "The children just want to get me into trouble."

"Open your mouth. Let me see!" cried Yasoda.

Krishna opened his mouth. Yasoda gazed inside. Time and space stood still. She gazed into the mouth of eternity. She saw the creation of Heaven and Earth. She saw the planets and the galaxies of the Universe. She saw earth, water, fire, and air. She saw volcanoes

SNAKE DEMON
Hindus believe *nagas* (sacred snakes) have the power to destroy. This is a painted wooden mask of a *naga rassa* (snake demon).

KRISHNA
Krishna's skin is usually shown as blue, the color of the sky and the oceans.

FESTIVAL OF HOLI
During Holi, people mimic Krishna's play with the cowherds' daughters.

and earthquakes, mountain ranges thrusting upward, rushing rivers, jungles, deserts, and shining oceans. She saw her own village and the herdsmen tending their flocks. She saw life and death.

Yasoda was gazing at creation itself in the mouth of Lord Vishnu. She understood that she didn't need to protect Krishna – he would protect her.

Krishna shut his mouth, and Yasoda immediately forgot everything she had seen. But her heart overflowed with love for him. She took him on her lap and was never afraid again.

MEENA'S SHRINE
Hindus worship daily, at home or in temples. Meena and her family often go to pray at this local shrine.

Yasoda saw all creation when she looked in Krishna's mouth.

Gulnara the Warrior

GULNARA AND HER SISTERS lived in a *ger* on the Mongolian plain with their father and one chestnut horse. One day a messenger ordered the men out to fight in the khan's army. Gulnara's father wrung his hands, "I'm an old man. I'd be no use."

Gulnara's father begged not to go to war.

"Too bad!" declared the messenger. "An order is an order. Obey, or the khan's men will slit your throat."

"Don't worry, Father!" cried his eldest daughter. "I will go in your place." She took her father's bow and sword, jumped on the chestnut's back, and galloped off.

She rode until she came to the Iron Mountain. Blocking her way was an evil black fox with a tail three leagues long. The chestnut reared in terror and raced back home.

"Let me go, Father!" said the second daughter. She took up the bow and sword, leaped upon the chestnut, and galloped off. She came to the Iron Mountain. Blocking her way was a huge wolf with a tail three leagues long. The chestnut horse reared with fright and galloped home. Father wailed. "This isn't woman's work. If I don't go, the khan's men will slit my throat."

Gulnara stepped forward. "I am the youngest, but I am taller and stronger than my sisters. I'm sure I'll get across the Iron Mountain." With bow and sword, Gulnara jumped onto the

ERDENE
Erdene lives in a remote area of Mongolia called Tsaluu, a grassy plain surrounded by hills. His family breeds horses, cows, sheep, and goats.

HORSEMAN
Like Gulnara, Erdene is a skilled horseman. He has his own horse, which he rides every day during the summer.

ERDENE'S HOME
Erdene lives in a traditional Mongolian home, a tent called a *ger*, as Gulnara did.

*A huge stag blocked
Gulnara's path.*

chestnut and galloped off. The
Iron Mountain rose before her.
Blocking the way was a huge
stag with six deadly antlers.
The horse pawed the air.

"Stay calm," murmured
Gulnara, "so I can fit an arrow
to my bow." Her soft words
quieted her steed. Gulnara fired.
Each arrow hit its mark. The dreadful creature crashed to the ground, dead.
Triumphantly, Gulnara entered the pass. The sky darkened. A huge swan
swept down. Gulnara fit an arrow, but the swan called, "Stop! I have come
to thank you for killing the stag and releasing me from his power. Take my
feather. It will give you my powers." A white feather spiraled to the ground.
Gulnara slid it in her shirt, then rode over the Iron Mountain.

The khan was feasting in
his iron tent when Gulnara
strode in.

*Gulnara strode into the
khan's tent without so much
as a nod to the khan.*

MAGIC ANIMALS
Mongolians thought
animals around them,
like the fox, wolf,
and stag reindeer, had
magic powers.

WOLF
Erdene
once saw
a wolf
when he
was out
herding. He
says, "I was very
scared, and I ran away."

CHINGHIS KHAN
The khan, or ruler, in
the story was probably
Chinghis Khan. In about
1200, he conquered an
empire stretching across
Asia from China to
Iran. Famed for his
cruelty, he could
severely punish
those who treated
him without
due respect.

Gulnara found the khan's army separated from the enemy by the waters of a thundering river.

THE KHAN'S ARMY Chinghis sent his army to wipe out rival Mongol rulers, such as Khan Kuzlun. His generals were often his own sons, or warriors hand-picked for their loyalty and determination.

"What lord are you, who does not bow before me?" he bellowed.

"I am no lord, just a maid, and I bow before no man. I have come to fight as you ordered."

"I asked for no woman. In any case, my armies have already left to fight Khan Kuzlun."

"Then I'd better catch up with them," declared Gulnara. She rode until nightfall, when she found the khan's army at a thundering river. On the other side was Khan Kuzlun's army. The generals were in despair. "How can we cross this river?" Gulnara pressed the swan's feather. Immediately, she turned into a swan, flew over the torrent, and landed outside Khan Kuzlun's tent.

Khan Kuzlun was talking to his wife, "We can cross the river by the horsehair bridge at the Iron Poplar Tree."

Mongol quiver

ARCHERY
Chinghis's mounted archers rode hardy Mongol horses, like Erdene's. Girls weren't supposed to fight, but Gulnara took no notice of this.

"What if the Great Khan's men find the bridge?"
"Then I will turn our armies into ashes, myself into a camel, you into iron, and our daughter into a silver birch."
Gulnara flew back to the other side and became a maid once more. She woke the generals and showed them where to cross the river. All they found at the enemy camp was a pile of ashes, a camel, a lump of iron, and a silver birch. "You've made a fool of us!" the generals roared.

Gulnara tied the camel to her horse's tail, put the lump of iron in her pocket, gathered the ashes into her saddle bag, and tucked the silver birch under her arm. Then she rode back and presented them to the khan. In an instant they were transformed. There stood Khan Kuzlun, his wife and daughter, and nine thousand soldiers. Everyone was amazed.
"Gulnara!" they cried. "What should we do?"
"Peace is better than war!" she replied. "Make friends."
So the khans made friends, and Gulnara galloped home on her chestnut horse.

SILVER BIRCH
Khan Kuzlun, his family, and army turn into everyday things that Mongolians thought were magic, such as trees and iron.

CAMELS
The camels that live in Mongolia are two-humped, Bactrian camels.

Gulnara presented the khan with the camel, the iron, the ashes, and the silver birch.

Rona and the Moon

ON THE NORTHERN SHORE of North Island, by a stretch of silver beach, lived a Maori woman named Rona. She lived with her husband and two sons – and what a happy life they led!

Every day Rona's husband and the other warriors took their canoes out fishing, while their young sons swam with the dolphins. Every evening Rona made sure the cooking stones were just hot enough to make a delicious meal of the fresh fish her husband would bring home.

Everything would have been perfect, but for one thing. Rona had such a bad temper. For no reason at all, she could fly off the handle. But her husband and children loved her all the same.

Rona would fly into a rage.

One summer's night the Moon was full and so bright that the fish rose to the surface of the sea, their silver scales flashing.

"This is a perfect night for fishing," said Rona's husband. "I will take the boys out with the warriors in the boat. We'll fish all night and all day tomorrow and be back the same time tomorrow night. We'll be starving, so make sure the cooking stones are just right so that we can cook our catch immediately."

Rona promised, thinking she would enjoy being alone for a while. She slept all

NGAWAIATA
Ngawaiata Evans lives on North Island in New Zealand. Her mother is Maori, and her name is a Maori word. Maoris were the first inhabitants of New Zealand.

SILVER BEACH
Like Rona, Ngawaiata lives near the beach. On fine days, she climbs her favorite tree to watch the dolphins swimming in the bay.

SUN STORY
At school Ngawaiata reads Maori stories, like *Rona and the Moon*, or the one in her book about a man who tries to catch the Sun.

night and didn't wake until the Sun was high. She meandered about all day, collecting wood for the fire and heating the cooking stones. From time to time, she dashed water on the stones. Nothing made her husband angrier than stones so hot they burned the fish.

The Sun dipped golden into the sea. The rising Moon mixed silver with gold. Dazzled, Rona fell into a dream.

"Heave ho! Home we go!"

The voices of father and sons rang through the night as their paddles cut into the water. Rona woke with a start. How long had she been asleep? Now there was no golden sunlight – just a dark sea and the silver Moon. She rushed over to her fire. It was burning brightly, but – oh, no! The cooking stones were blazing hot. She hadn't cooled them for hours and both water gourds were empty.

"Heave ho!" The voices were nearer, hungry and eager to get home for that delicious fish dinner. Panic-stricken, Rona grabbed the gourds and ran toward the spring.

It was a rocky path and uphill all the way.

After her day's work, Rona fell into a dreamy sleep.

Mussel fritter

Shellfish

Scones

SEAFOOD Ngawaiata's family, like Rona's, eats fish and shellfish from the bay. Rona cooks the traditional Maori way: heating stones to bake fish over in an earth oven.

Edible John Dory fish

*Rona fell and
spilled the water.*

She scrambled and stumbled, but reached the spring and filled her gourds to the brim. Heaving one on each hip, she set off back down the path. At the steepest point, the Moon disappeared behind a cloud, plunging Rona into darkness. She tripped and fell. Her gourds smashed. The water sloshed out. Bashed and bruised, Rona scrambled to her feet. Mockingly, out came the Moon again.

"You blithering idiot! You useless piece of rock in the sky! Look what you made me do by hiding your light!" she screamed her insults.

"Pokokuhua, cooked head!"

The Moon was usually a calm sort of body, drifting above the petty affairs of life, but Rona's insults were too much. It spun down out of the sky and, before she could say "pokokuhua" one more time, swept her upward.

"Oh, no, you don't!" shrieked Rona, grabbing the branches of a ngaio tree and hanging on for dear life.

"Oh, yes, I do!" boomed the Moon and, with one more mighty tug, yanked Rona into the heavens.

When father and sons returned, they found a blazing fire, and stones too hot for cooking. But where was Rona?

They searched from sunrise to sunset, shouting her name. Darkness fell. They collapsed exhausted on the ground and stared up at the starry sky.

"The Moon! Look at

STRONG SEAMEN
Maoris were expert sailors. Rona's family and the warriors paddled canoes miles across the ocean on fishing trips. Ngawaiata loves to go sailing with her father.

*Canoe bailer
for scooping
out water*

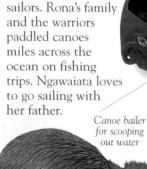

KIWI
"Kiwi" is the Maori name for New Zealand's most famous bird, which feeds by moon-light.

Kowhai tree

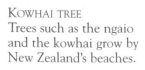

KOWHAI TREE
Trees such as the ngaio and the kowhai grow by New Zealand's beaches.

the Moon!" they cried.

On the glistening orb was the shape of a woman clasping two gourds, one under each arm. Rona must have cursed once too often. Now she was doomed to float through the skies forever and ever.

"Kia mahara ki te he o Rona," say the Maoris. "Remember what happened to Rona."

The Moon swept Rona up into the sky.

MOON DWELLERS
People all over the world think they see someone in the Moon. For Maoris, it is Rona. In many places, people speak of the Man in the Moon.